THE

THE HAUNTED BOOKSHELF

he telling or reading of ghost stories during long, dark, and cold Christmas nights is a yuletide ritual dating back to at least the eighteenth century, and was once as much a part of Christmas tradition as decorating fir trees, feasting on goose, and the singing of carols. During the Victorian era many magazines printed ghost stories specifically for the Christmas season. These "winter tales" didn't necessarily explore Christmas themes. Rather, they were offered as an eerie pleasure to be enjoyed on Christmas eve with the family, adding a supernatural shiver to the seasonal chill.

The tradition remained strong in the British Isles (and her colonies) throughout much of the twentieth century, though in recent years it has been on the wane. Certainly, few people in Canada or the United States seem to know about it any longer. This series of small books seeks to rectify this, to revive a charming custom for the long, dark nights we all know so well here at Christmastime.

THE HAUNTED BOOKSHELF

THE APPLE TREE

THE
APPLE
TREE

DAPHNE DU MAURIER

A GHOST STORY FOR
CHRISTMAS

DESIGNED & DECORATED BY SETH

BIBLIOASIS

I t was three months after she died that he first noticed the apple tree. He had known of its existence, of course, with the others, standing upon the lawn in front of the house, sloping upwards to the field beyond. Never before, though, had he been aware of this particular tree looking in any way different from its fellows, except that it was the third one on the left, a little apart from the rest and leaning more closely to the terrace. It was a fine clear morning in early spring, and he was shaving by the open window. As he leant out to sniff the air, the lather on his face, the razor in his hand, his eye fell upon the apple tree. It was a trick of light, perhaps, something to do with the sun coming up over the woods, that happened to catch the tree at this particular moment; but the likeness was unmistakable.

He put his razor down on the window ledge and stared. The tree was scraggy and of a depressing thinness, possessing none of the gnarled solidity of its companions. Its few branches, growing high up on the trunk like narrow shoulders on a tall body, spread themselves in martyred resignation, as though chilled by the fresh morning air. The roll of wire circling the tree, and reaching to about halfway up the trunk from the base, looked like a grey tweed skirt covering lean limbs; while the topmost branch, sticking up into the air above the ones below, yet sagging slightly, could have been a drooping head poked forward in an attitude of weariness.

How often he had seen Midge stand like this, dejected. No matter where it was, whether in the garden, or in the house, or even shopping in the town, she would take upon herself this same stooping posture, suggesting that life treated her hardly, that she had been singled out from her fellows to carry some impossible burden, but in spite of it would endure to the end without complaint. 'Midge, you look worn out, for heaven's sake sit down and take a rest!' But the words would be received with the inevitable shrug of the shoulder, the inevitable sigh, 'Someone has got to keep things going,' and straightening herself she would embark upon the dreary routine of unnecessary tasks she forced herself to do, day in, day out, through the interminable changeless years.

He went on staring at the apple tree. That martyred bent position, the stooping top, the weary branches, the few withered leaves that had not blown away with the wind and rain of the past winter and now shivered in the spring breeze like wispy hair; all of it protested soundlessly to the owner of the garden looking upon it, 'I am like this because of you, because of your neglect.' He turned away from the window and went on shaving. It would not do to let his imagination run away with him and start building fancies in his mind just when he was settling at long last to freedom. He bathed and dressed and went down to breakfast. Egg and bacon were waiting for him on the hot plate, and he carried the dish to the single place laid for him at the dining table. *The Times*, folded smooth and new, was ready for him to read. When Midge was alive he had handed it to her first, from long custom, and when she gave it back to him after breakfast, to take with him to the study, the pages were always in the wrong order and folded crookedly, so that part of the pleasure of reading it was spoilt. The news, too, would be stale to him after she had read the worst of it aloud, which was a morning habit she used to take upon herself, always adding some derogatory remark of her own about what she read. The birth of a daughter to mutual friends would bring a click of the tongue, a little jerk of the head, 'Poor things, another girl,' or if a son, 'A boy can't be much fun to educate these days.' He used to think it psychological, because they themselves were childless, that she should so grudge the entry of new life into the world; but as time passed it became thus with all bright or joyous things, as though there was some fundamental blight upon good cheer.

'It says here that more people went on holiday this year than ever before. Let's hope they enjoyed themselves, that's all.' But no hope lay in her words, only disparagement. Then, having finished breakfast, she would push back her chair and sigh and say, 'Oh well . . .,' leaving the sentence unfinished; but the sigh, the shrug of the shoulders, the slope of her long, thin back as she stooped to clear the dishes from the serving-table—thus sparing work for the daily maid—was all part of her long-term reproach, directed at him, that had marred their existence over a span of years.

Silent, punctilious, he would open the door for her to pass through to the kitchen quarters, and she would labour past him, stooping under the weight of the laden tray that there was no need for her to carry, and presently, through the half-open door, he would hear the swish of the running water from the pantry tap. He would return to his chair and sit down again, the crumpled *Times*, a smear of marmalade upon it, lying against the toast-rack; and once again, with monotonous insistence, the question hammered at his mind, 'What have I done?'

It was not as though she nagged. Nagging wives, like mothers-in-law, were chestnut jokes for music halls. He could not remember Midge ever losing her temper or quarrelling. It was just that the undercurrent of reproach, mingled with suffering nobly borne, spoilt the atmosphere of his home and drove him to a sense of furtiveness and guilt.

Perhaps it would be raining and he, seeking sanctuary within his study, electric fire aglow, his after-breakfast pipe filling the small room with smoke, would settle down before his desk in a pretence of writing letters, but in reality to hide, to feel the snug security of four safe walls that were his alone. Then the door would open and Midge, struggling into a raincoat, her wide-brimmed felt hat pulled low over her brow, would pause and wrinkle her nose in distaste.

'Phew! What a fug.'

He said nothing, but moved slightly in his chair, covering with his arm the novel he had chosen from a shelf in idleness.

'Aren't you going into the town?' she asked him.

'I had not thought of doing so.'

'Oh! Oh, well, it doesn't matter.' She turned away again towards the door.

'Why, is there anything you want done?'

'It's only the fish for lunch. They don't deliver on Wednesdays.

Still, I can go myself if you are busy. I only thought . . .' She was out of the room without finishing her sentence.

'It's all right, Midge,' he called, 'I'll get the car and go and fetch it presently. No sense in getting wet.'

Thinking she had not heard he went out into the hall. She was standing by the open front door, the mizzling rain driving in upon her. She had a long flat basket over her arm and was drawing on a pair of gardening gloves.

'I'm bound to get wet in any case,' she said, 'so it doesn't make much odds. Look at those flowers, they all need staking. I'll go for the fish when I've finished seeing to them.'

Argument was useless. She had made up her mind. He shut the front door after her and sat down again in the study. Somehow the room no longer felt so snug, and a little later, raising his head to the window, he saw her hurry past, her raincoat not buttoned properly and flapping, little drips of water forming on the brim of her hat and the garden basket filled with limp michaelmas daisies already dead. His conscience pricking him, he bent down and turned out one bar of the electric fire.

Or yet again it would be spring, it would be summer. Strolling out hatless into the garden, his hands in his pockets, with no other purpose in his mind but to feel the sun upon his back and stare out upon the woods and fields and the slow winding river, he would hear, from the bedrooms above, the high-pitched whine

of the Hoover slow down suddenly, gasp, and die. Midge called down to him as he stood there on the terrace.

'Were you going to do anything?' she said.

He was not. It was the smell of spring, of early summer, that had driven him out into the garden. It was the delicious knowledge that being retired now, no longer working in the City, time was a thing of no account, he could waste it as he pleased.

'No,' he said, 'not on such a lovely day. Why?'

'Oh, never mind,' she answered, 'it's only that the wretched drain under the kitchen window has gone wrong again. Completely plugged up and choked. No one ever sees to it, that's why. I'll have a go at it myself this afternoon.'

Her face vanished from the window. Once more there was a gasp, a rising groan of sound, and the Hoover warmed to its task again. What foolishness that such an interruption could damp the brightness of the day. Not the demand, nor the task itself—clearing a drain was in its own way a schoolboy piece of folly, playing with mud—but that wan face of hers looking out upon the sunlit terrace, the hand that went up wearily to push back a strand of falling hair, and the inevitable sigh before she turned from the window, the unspoken, 'I wish I had the time to stand and do nothing in the sun. Oh, well . . .'

He had ventured to ask once why so much cleaning of the house was necessary. Why there must be the incessant turning out of rooms. Why chairs must be lifted to stand upon other chairs, rugs rolled up and ornaments huddled together on a sheet of newspaper. And why, in particular, the sides of the upstairs corridor, on which no one ever trod, must be polished laboriously by hand, Midge and the daily woman taking it in turns to crawl upon their knees the whole endless length of it, like slaves of bygone days.

Midge stared at him, not understanding.

'You'd be the first to complain,' she said, 'if the house was like a pigsty. You like your comforts.'

So they lived in different worlds, their minds not meeting. Had it been always so? He did not remember. They had been married nearly twenty-five years and were two people who, from force of habit, lived under the same roof.

When he had been in business, it seemed different. He had not noticed it so much. He came home to eat, to sleep, and to go up by train again in the morning. But when he retired he became aware of her forcibly, and day by day his sense of her resentment, of her disapproval, grew stronger.

Finally, in that last year before she died, he felt himself engulfed in it, so that he was led into every sort of petty deception to get away from her, making a pretence of going up to London to have his hair cut, to see the dentist, to lunch with an old business friend; and in reality he would be sitting by his club window, anonymous, at peace.

It was mercifully swift, the illness that took her from him. Influenza, followed by pneumonia, and she was dead within a week. He hardly knew how it happened, except that as usual she was overtired and caught a cold, and would not stay in bed. One evening, coming home by the late train from London, having sneaked into a cinema during the afternoon, finding release amongst the crowd of warm friendly people enjoying themselves—for it was a bitter December day—he found her bent over the furnace in the cellar, poking and thrusting at the lumps of coke.

She looked up at him, white with fatigue, her face drawn. 'Why, Midge, what on earth are you doing?' he said.

'It's the furnace,' she said, 'we've had trouble with it all day, it won't stay alight. We shall have to get the men to see it tomorrow. I really cannot manage this sort of thing myself.'

There was a streak of coal dust on her cheek. She let the stubby poker fall on the cellar floor. She began to cough, and as she did so winced with pain.

'You ought to be in bed,' he said, 'I never heard of such nonsense. What the dickens does it matter about the furnace?'

'I thought you would be home early,' she said, 'and then you might have known how to deal with it. It's been bitter all day, I can't think what you found to do with yourself in London.'

She climbed the cellar stairs slowly, her back bent, and when she reached the top she stood shivering and half closed her eyes. 'If you don't mind terribly,' she said, 'I'll get your supper right away, to have it done with. I don't want anything myself.'

'To hell with my supper,' he said, 'I can forage for myself. You go up to bed. I'll bring you a hot drink.'

'I tell you, I don't want anything,' she said. 'I can fill my hot-water bottle myself. I only ask one thing of you. And that is to remember to turn out the lights every-where, before you come up.' She turned into the hall, her shoulders sagging.

'Surely a glass of hot milk?' he began uncertainly, starting to take off his over-coat; and as he did so the torn half of the ten-and-sixpenny seat at the cinema fell from his pocket on to the floor. She saw it. She said nothing. She coughed again and began to drag herself upstairs.

The next morning her temperature was a hundred and three. The doctor came and said she had pneumonia. She asked if she might go to a private ward in the cottage hospital, because having a nurse in the house would make too much work. This was on the Tuesday morning. She went there right away, and they told him on the Friday evening that she was not likely to live through the night. He stood inside the room, after they told him, looking down at her in the high impersonal hospital bed, and his heart was wrung with pity, because surely they had given her too many pillows, she was propped too high, there could be no rest for her that way. He had brought some flowers, but there seemed no purpose now in giving them to the nurse to arrange, because Midge was too ill to look at them. In a sort of delicacy he put them on a table beside the screen, when the nurse was bending down to her.

'Is there anything she needs?' he said. 'I mean, I can easily . . .' He did not finish the sentence, he left it in the air, hoping the nurse would understand his intention, that he was ready to go off in the car, drive somewhere, fetch what was required.

The nurse shook her head. 'We will telephone you,' she said, 'if there is any change.'

What possible change could there be, he wondered, as he found himself outside the hospital? The white pinched face upon the pillows would not alter now, it belonged to no one.

Midge died in the early hours of Saturday morning.

He was not a religious man, he had no profound belief in immortality, but when the funeral was over, and Midge was buried, it distressed him to think of her poor lonely body lying in that brand-new coffin with the brass handles: it seemed such a churlish thing to permit. Death should be different. It should be like bidding farewell to someone at a station before a long journey, but without the strain. There was something of indecency in this haste to bury underground the thing that but for ill-chance would be a living breathing person. In his distress he fancied he could hear Midge saying with a sigh, 'Oh, well . . .' as they lowered the coffin into the open grave.

He hoped with fervour that after all there might be a future in some unseen Paradise and that poor Midge, unaware of what they were doing to her mortal remains, walked somewhere in green fields. But who with, he wondered? Her parents had died in India many years ago; she would not have much in common with them now if they met her at the gates of Heaven. He had a sudden picture of her waiting her turn in a queue, rather far back, as was always her fate in queues, with that large shopping bag of woven straw which she took everywhere, and on her face that patient martyred look. As she passed through the turnstile into Paradise she looked at him, reproachfully.

These pictures, of the coffin and the queue, remained with him for about a week, fading a little day by day. Then he forgot her. Freedom was his, and the sunny empty house, the bright crisp winter. The routine he followed belonged to him alone. He never thought of Midge until the morning he looked out upon the apple tree.

Later that day he was taking a stroll round the garden, and he found himself drawn to the tree through curiosity. It had been stupid fancy after all. There was nothing singular about it. An apple tree like any other apple tree. He remembered then that it had always been a poorer tree than its fellows, was in fact more than half-dead, and at one time there had been talk of chopping it down, but the talk came to nothing. Well, it would be something for him to do over the weekend. Axing a tree was healthy exercise, and apple wood smelt good. It would be a treat to have it burning on the fire.

Unfortunately wet weather set in for nearly a week after that day, and he was unable to accomplish the task he had set himself. No sense in pottering out of doors in this weather, and getting a chill into the bargain. He still noticed the tree from his bedroom window. It began to irritate him, humped there, straggling and thin, under the rain. The weather was not cold, and the rain that fell upon the garden was soft and gentle. None of the other trees wore this aspect of dejection. There was one young tree—only planted a few years back, he recalled quite well—growing to the right of the old one and standing straight and firm, the lithe young branches lifted to the sky, positively looking as if it enjoyed the rain. He peered through the window at it, and smiled. Now why the devil should he suddenly remember that incident, years back, during the war, with the girl who came to work on the land for a few months at the neighbouring farm? He did not suppose he had thought of her in months. Besides, there was nothing to it. At weekends he had helped them at the farm himself—war work of a sort—and she was always there, cheerful and pretty and smiling; she had dark curling hair, crisp and boyish, and a skin like a very young apple.

He looked forward to seeing her, Saturdays and Sundays; it was an antidote to the inevitable news bulletins put on throughout the day by Midge, and to ceaseless war talk. He liked looking at the child—she was scarcely more than that, nineteen or so—in her slim breeches and gay shirts; and when she smiled it was as though she embraced the world.

He never knew how it happened, and it was such a little thing; but one afternoon he was in the shed doing something to the tractor, bending over the engine, and she was beside him, close to his shoulder, and they were laughing together; and he turned round, to take a bit of waste to clean a plug, and suddenly she was in his arms and he was kissing her. It was a happy thing, spontaneous and free, and the girl so warm and jolly, with her fresh young mouth. Then they went on with the work of the tractor, but united now, in a kind of intimacy that brought gaiety to them both, and peace as well. When it was time for the girl to go and feed the pigs he followed her from the shed, his hand on her shoulder, a careless gesture that meant nothing really, a half-caress; and as they came out into the yard he saw Midge standing there, staring at them.

'I've got to go in to a Red Cross meeting,' she said. 'I can't get the car to start. I called you. You didn't seem to hear.'

Her face was frozen. She was looking at the girl. At once guilt covered him. The girl said good evening cheerfully to Midge, and crossed the yard to the pigs.

He went with Midge to the car and managed to start it with the handle. Midge thanked him, her voice without expression. He found himself unable to meet her eyes. This, then, was adultery. This was sin. This was the second page in a Sunday newspaper—'Husband Intimate with Land Girl in Shed. Wife Witnesses Act.' His hands were shaking when he got back to the house and he had to pour himself a drink. Nothing was ever said. Midge never mentioned the matter. Some craven instinct kept him from the farm the next weekend, and then he heard that the girl's mother had been taken ill and she had been called back home. He never saw her again. Why, he wondered, should he remember her suddenly, on such a day, watching the rain falling on the apple trees? He must certainly make a point of cutting down the old dead tree, if only for the sake of bringing more sunshine to the little sturdy one; it hadn't a fair chance, growing there so close to the other.

On Friday afternoon he went round to the vegetable garden to find Willis, the jobbing gardener, who came three days a week, to pay him his wages. He wanted, too, to look in the toolshed and see if the axe and saw were in good condition. Willis kept everything neat and tidy there—this was Midge's training—and the axe and saw were hanging in their accustomed place upon the wall.

He paid Willis his money, and was turning away when the man suddenly said to him, 'Funny thing, sir, isn't it, about the old apple tree?'

The remark was so unexpected that it came as a shock. He felt himself change colour.

'Apple tree? What apple tree?' he said.

'Why, the one at the far end, near the terrace,' answered Willis. 'Been barren as long as I've worked here, and that's some years now. Never an apple from her, nor as much as a sprig of blossom. We were going to chop her up that cold winter, if you remember, and we never did. Well, she's taken on a new lease now. Haven't you noticed?' The gardener watched him smiling, a knowing look in his eye.

What did the fellow mean? It was not possible that he had been struck also by that fantastic freak resemblance—no, it was out of the question, indecent, blasphemous; besides, he had put it out of his own mind now, he had not thought of it again.

'I've noticed nothing,' he said, on the defensive.

Willis laughed. 'Come round to the terrace, sir,' he said, 'I'll show you.'

They went together to the sloping lawn, and when they came to the apple tree Willis put his hand up and pulled down a branch within reach. It creaked a little as he did so, as though stiff and unyielding, and Willis brushed away some of the dry lichen and revealed the spiky twigs. 'Look there, sir,' he said, 'she's growing buds. Look at them, feel them for yourself. There's life here yet, and plenty of it. Never known such a thing before. See this branch too.' He released the first, and leant up to reach another. Willis was right. There were buds in plenty, but so small and brown that it seemed to him they scarcely deserved the name, they were more like blemishes upon the twig, dusty and dry. He put his hands in his pockets. He felt a queer distaste to touch them.

'I don't think they'll amount to much,' he said.

'I don't know, sir,' said Willis, 'I've got hopes. She's stood the winter, and if we get no more bad frosts there's no knowing what we'll see. It would be some joke to watch the old tree blossom. She'll bear fruit yet.' He patted the trunk with his open hand, in a gesture at once familiar and affectionate.

The owner of the apple tree turned away. For some reason he felt irritated with Willis. Anyone would think the damned tree lived. And now his plan to axe the tree, over the weekend, would come to nothing.

'It's taking the light from the young tree,' he said. 'Surely it would be more to the point if we did away with this one, and gave the little one more room?'

He moved across to the young tree and touched a limb. No lichen here. The branches smooth. Buds upon every twig, curling tight. He let go the branch and it sprang away from him, resilient. 'Do away with her, sir,' said Willis, 'while there's still life in her? Oh no, sir, I wouldn't do that. She's doing no harm to the young tree. I'd give the old tree one more chance. If she doesn't bear fruit, we'll have her down next winter.'

'All right, Willis,' he said, and walked swiftly away. Somehow he did not want to discuss the matter any more.

That night, when he went to bed, he opened the window wide as usual and drew back the curtains; he could not bear to wake up in the morning and find the room close. It was full moon, and the light shone down upon the terrace and the lawn above it, ghostly pale and still. No wind blew. A hush upon the place. He leant out, loving the silence. The moon shone full upon the little apple tree, the young one. There was a radiance about it in this light that gave it a fairy-tale quality. Small and lithe and slim, the young tree might have been a dancer, her arms upheld, poised ready on her toes for flight. Such a careless, happy grace about it. Brave young tree. Away to the left stood the other one, half of it in shadow still. Even the moonlight could not give it beauty. What in heaven's name was the matter with the thing that it had to stand there, humped and stooping, instead of looking upwards to the light? It marred the still quiet night, it spoilt the setting. He had been a fool to give way to Willis and agree to spare the tree. Those ridiculous buds would never blossom, and even if they did . . .

His thoughts wandered, and for the second time that week he found himself remembering the landgirl and her joyous smile. He wondered what had happened to her. Married probably, with a young family. Made some chap happy, no doubt. Oh, well . . . He smiled. Was he going to make use of that expression now? Poor Midge! Then he caught his breath and stood quite still, his hand upon the curtain. The apple tree, the one on the left, was no longer in shadow. The moon shone upon the withered branches, and they looked like skeleton's arms raised in supplication. Frozen arms, stiff and numb with pain. There was no wind, and the other trees were motionless; but there, in those topmost branches, something shivered and stirred, a breeze that came from nowhere and died away again. Suddenly a branch fell from the apple tree to the ground below. It was the near branch, with the small dark buds upon it, which he would not touch. No rustle, no breath of movement came from the other trees. He went on staring at the branch as it lay there on the grass, under the moon. It stretched across the shadow of the young tree close to it, pointing as though in accusation.

For the first time in his life that he could remember he drew the curtains over the window to shut out the light of the moon.

Willis was supposed to keep to the vegetable garden. He had never shown his face much round the front when Midge was alive. That was because Midge attended to the flowers. She even used to mow the grass, pushing the wretched machine up and down the slope, her back bent low over the handles.

It had been one of the tasks she set herself, like keeping the bedrooms swept and polished. Now Midge was no longer there to attend to the front garden and to tell him where he should work, Willis was always coming through to the front. The gardener liked the change. It made him feel responsible.

'I can't understand how that branch came to fall, sir,' he said on the Monday.

'What branch?'

'Why, the branch on the apple tree. The one we were looking at before I left.'

'It was rotten, I suppose. I told you the tree was dead.'

'Nothing rotten about it, sir. Why, look at it. Broke clean off.' Once again the owner was obliged to follow his man up the slope above the terrace. Willis picked up the branch. The lichen upon it was wet, bedraggled looking, like matted hair.

'You didn't come again to test the branch, over the weekend, and loosen it in some fashion, did you, sir?' asked the gardener.

'I most certainly did not,' replied the owner, irritated. 'As a matter of fact I heard the branch fall, during the night. I was opening the bedroom window at the time.'

'Funny. It was a still night too.'

'These things often happen to old trees. Why you bother about this one I can't imagine. Anyone would think . . .'

He broke off; he did not know how to finish the sentence. 'Anyone would think that the tree was valuable,' he said.

The gardener shook his head. 'It's not the value,' he said. 'I don't reckon for a moment that this tree is worth any money at all. It's just that after all this time, when we thought her dead, she's alive and kicking, as you might say. Freak of nature, I call it. We'll hope no other branches fall before she blossoms.'

Later, when the owner set off for his afternoon walk, he saw the man cutting away the grass below the tree and placing new wire around the base of the trunk. It was quite ridiculous. He did not pay the fellow a fat wage to tinker about with a half-dead tree. He ought to be in the kitchen garden, growing vegetables. It was too much effort, though, to argue with him.

He returned home about half past five. Tea was a discarded meal since Midge had died, and he was looking forward to his armchair by the fire, his pipe, his whisky-and-soda, and silence. The fire had not long been lit and the chimney was smoking.

There was a queer, rather sickly smell about the living room. He threw open the windows and went upstairs to change his heavy shoes. When he came down again the smoke still clung about the room and the smell was as strong as ever. Impossible to name it. Sweetish, strange. He called to the woman out in the kitchen.

'There's a funny smell in the house,' he said. 'What is it?' The woman came out into the hall from the back. 'What sort of a smell, sir?' she said, on the defensive.

'It's in the living room,' he said. 'The room was full of smoke just now. Have you been burning something?'

Her face cleared. 'It must be the logs,' she said. 'Willis cut them up specially, sir, he said you would like them.'

'What logs are those?'

'He said it was apple wood, sir, from a branch he had sawed up. Apple wood burns well, I've always heard. Some people fancy it very much. I don't notice any smell myself, but I've got a slight cold.'

Together they looked at the fire. Willis had cut the logs small. The woman, thinking to please him, had piled several on top of one another, to make a good fire to last. There was no great blaze. The smoke that came from them was thin and poor. Greenish in colour. Was it possible she did not notice that sickly rancid smell? 'The logs are wet,' he said abruptly. 'Willis should have known better. Look at them. Quite useless on my fire.'

The woman's face took on a set, rather sulky expression. 'I'm very sorry,' she said. 'I didn't notice anything wrong with them when I came to light the fire. They seemed to start well. I've always understood apple wood was very good for burning, and Willis said the same. He told me to be sure and see that you had these on the fire this evening, he had made a special job of cutting them for you. I thought you knew about it and had given orders.'

'Oh, all right,' he answered, abruptly. 'I dare say they'll burn in time. It's not your fault.'

He turned his back on her and poked at the fire, trying to separate the logs.

While she remained in the house there was nothing he could do. To remove the damp smouldering logs and throw them somewhere round the back, and then light the fire afresh with dry sticks would arouse comment. He would have to go through the kitchen to the back passage where the kindling wood was kept, and she would stare at him, and come forward and say, 'Let me do it, sir. Has the fire gone out then?' No, he must wait until after supper, when she had cleared away and washed up and gone off for the night. Meanwhile, he would endure the smell of the apple wood as best he could.

He poured out his drink, lit his pipe and stared at the fire. It gave out no heat at all, and with the central heating off in the house the living room struck chill. Now and again a thin wisp of the greenish smoke puffed from the logs, and with it seemed to come that sweet sickly smell, unlike any sort of wood smoke that he knew. That interfering fool of a gardener . . . Why saw up the logs? He must have known they were damp. Riddled with damp. He leant forward, staring more closely. Was it damp, though, that oozed there in a thin trickle from the pale logs? No, it was sap, unpleasant, slimy.

He seized the poker, and in a fit of irritation thrust it between the logs, trying to stir them to flame, to change that green smoke into a normal blaze. The effort was useless. The logs would not burn. And all the while the trickle of sap ran on to the grate and the sweet smell filled the room, turning his stomach. He took his glass and his book and went and turned on the electric fire in the study and sat in there instead.

It was idiotic. It reminded him of the old days, how he would make a pretence of writing letters, and go and sit in the study because of Midge in the living room. She had a habit of yawning in the evenings, when her day's work was done; a habit of which she was quite unconscious. She would settle herself on the sofa with her knitting, the click-click of the needles going fast and furious; and suddenly they would start, those shattering yawns, rising from the depths of her, a prolonged 'Ah . . . Ah . . . Hi-Oh!' followed by the inevitable sigh. Then there would be silence except for the knitting needles, but as he sat behind his book, waiting, he knew that within a few minutes another yawn would come, another sigh. A hopeless sort of anger used to stir within him, a longing to throw down his book and say, 'Look, if you are so tired, wouldn't it be better if you went to bed?'

Instead, he controlled himself, and after a little while, when he could bear it no longer, he would get up and leave the living room, and take refuge in the study. Now he was doing the same thing, all over again, because of the apple logs. Because of the damned sickly smell of the smouldering wood.

He went on sitting in his chair by the desk, waiting for supper. It was nearly nine o'clock before the daily woman had cleared up, turned down his bed and gone for the night.

He returned to the living room, which he had not entered since leaving it earlier in the evening. The fire was out. It had made some effort to burn, because the logs were thinner than they had been before, and had sunk low into the basket grate. The ash was meagre, yet the sickly smell clung to the dying embers. He went out into the kitchen and found an empty scuttle and brought it back into the living room. Then he lifted the logs into it, and the ashes too. There must have been some damp residue in the scuttle, or the logs were still not dry, because as they settled there they seemed to turn darker than before, with a kind of scum upon them. He carried the scuttle down to the cellar, opened the door of the central heating furnace, and threw the lot inside.

He remembered then, too late, that the central heating had been given up now for two or three weeks, owing to the spring weather, and that unless he relit it now the logs would remain there, untouched, until the following winter. He found paper, matches, and a can of paraffin, and setting the whole alight closed the door of the furnace, and listened to the roar of flames. That would settle it. He waited a moment and then went up the steps, back to the kitchen passage, to lay and relight the fire in the living room. The business took time, he had to find kindling and coal, but with patience he got the new fire started, and finally settled himself down in his arm-chair before it.

He had been reading perhaps for twenty minutes before he became aware of the banging door. He put down his book and listened. Nothing at first. Then, yes, there it was again. A rattle, a slam of an unfastened door in the kitchen quarters.

He got up and went along to shut it. It was the door at the top of the cellar stairs. He could have sworn he had fastened it. The catch must have worked loose in some way. He switched on the light at the head of the stairs, and bent to examine the catch. There seemed nothing wrong with it. He was about to close the door firmly when he noticed the smell again. The sweet sickly smell of smouldering apple wood. It was creeping up from the cellar, finding its way to the passage above.

Suddenly, for no reason, he was seized with a kind of fear, a feeling of panic almost. What if the smell filled the whole house through the night, came up from the kitchen quarters to the floor above, and while he slept found its way into his bedroom, choking him, stifling him, so that he could not breathe? The thought was ridiculous, insane—and yet . . .

Once more he forced himself to descend the steps into the cellar. No sound came from the furnace, no roar of flames. Wisps of smoke, thin and green, oozed their way from the fastened furnace door; it was this that he had noticed from the passage above.

He went to the furnace and threw open the door. The paper had all burnt away, and the few shavings with them. But the logs, the apple logs, had not burnt at all. They lay there as they had done when he threw them in, one charred limb above another, black and huddled, like the bones of someone darkened and dead by fire. Nausea rose in him. He thrust his handkerchief into his mouth, choking. Then, scarcely knowing what he did, he ran up the steps to find the empty scuttle, and with a shovel and tongs tried to pitch the logs back into it, scraping for them through the narrow door of the furnace. He was retching in his belly all the while. At last the scuttle was filled, and he carried it up the steps and through the kitchen to the back door.

He opened the door. Tonight there was no moon and it was raining. Turning up the collar of his coat he peered about him in the darkness, wondering where he should throw the logs. Too wet and dark to stagger all the way to the kitchen garden and chuck them on the rubbish heap, but in the field behind the garage the grass was thick and long and they might lie there hidden. He crunched his way over the gravel drive, and coming to the fence beside the field threw his burden on to the concealing grass. There they could rot and perish, grow sodden with rain, and in the end become part of the mouldy earth; he did not care. The responsibility was his no longer. They were out of his house, and it did not matter what became of them.

He returned to the house, and this time made sure the cellar door was fast. The air was clear again, the smell had gone.

He went back to the living room to warm himself before the fire, but his hands and feet, wet with the rain, and his stomach, still queasy from the pungent smoke, combined together to chill his whole person, and he sat there, shuddering.

He slept badly when he went to bed that night, and awoke in the morning feeling out of sorts. He had a headache, and an ill-tasting tongue. He stayed indoors. His liver was thoroughly upset. To relieve his feelings he spoke sharply to the daily woman. 'I've caught a bad chill,' he said to her, 'trying to get warm last night. So much for apple wood. The smell of it has affected my inside as well. You can tell Willis, when he comes tomorrow.'

She looked at him in disbelief.

'I'm sure I'm very sorry,' she said. 'I told my sister about the wood last night, when I got home, and that you had not fancied it. She said it was most unusual. Apple wood is considered quite a luxury to burn, and burns well, what's more.'

'This lot didn't, that's all I know,' he said to her, 'and I never want to see any more of it. As for the smell . . . I can taste it still, it's completely turned me up.'

Her mouth tightened. 'I'm sorry,' she said. And then, as she left the dining room, her eye fell on the empty whisky bottle on the sideboard. She hesitated a moment, then put it on her tray.

'You've finished with this, sir?' she said.

Of course he had finished with it. It was obvious. The bottle was empty. He realized the implication, though. She wanted to suggest that the idea of applewood smoke upsetting him was all my eye, he had done himself too well. Damned impertinence.

'Yes,' he said, 'you can bring another in its place.' That would teach her to mind her own business.

He was quite sick for several days, queasy and giddy, and finally rang up the doctor to come and have a look at him. The story of the applewood sounded nonsense, when he told it, and the doctor, after examining him, appeared unimpressed.

'Just a chill on the liver,' he said, 'damp feet, and possibly something you've eaten combined. I hardly think wood smoke has much to do with it. You ought to take more exercise, if you're inclined to have a liver. Play golf. I don't know how I should keep fit without my weekend golf.' He laughed, packing up his bag. 'I'll make you up some medicine,' he said, 'and once this rain has cleared off I should get out and into the air. It's mild enough, and all we want now is a bit of sunshine to bring everything on. Your garden is farther ahead than mine. Your fruit trees are ready to blossom.' And then, before leaving the room, he added, 'You mustn't forget, you had a bad shock a few months ago. It takes time to get over these things. You're still missing your wife, you know. Best thing is to get out and about and see people. Well, take care of yourself.'

His patient dressed and went downstairs. The fellow meant well, of course, but his visit had been a waste of time. 'You're still missing your wife, you know.' How little the doctor understood. Poor Midge ... At least he himself had the honesty to admit that he did not miss her at all, that now she was gone he could breathe, he was free, and that apart from the upset liver he had not felt so well for years.

During the few days he had spent in bed the daily woman had taken the opportunity to spring clean the living room. An unnecessary piece of work, but he supposed it was part of the legacy Midge had left behind her. The room looked scrubbed and straight and much too tidy. His own personal litter cleared, books and papers neatly stacked. It was an infernal nuisance, really, having anyone to do for him at all. It would not take much for him to sack her and fend for himself as best he could. Only the bother, the time of cooking and washing up, prevented him. The ideal life, of course, was that led by a man out East, or in the South Seas, who took a native wife.

No problem there. Silence, good service, perfect waiting, excellent cooking, no need for conversation; and then, if you wanted something more than that, there she was, young, warm, a companion for the dark hours. No criticism ever, the obedience of an animal to its master, and the light-hearted laughter of a child. Yes, they had wisdom all right, those fellows who broke away from convention. Good luck to them.

He strolled over to the window and looked out up the sloping lawn. The rain was stopping and tomorrow it would be fine; he would be able to get out, as the doctor had suggested. The man was right, too, about the fruit trees. The little one near the steps was in flower already, and a blackbird had perched himself on one of the branches, which swayed slightly under his weight.

The raindrops glistened and the opening buds were very curled and pink, but when the sun broke through tomorrow they would turn white and soft against the blue of the sky. He must find his old camera, and put a film in it, and photograph the little tree. The others would be in flower, too, during the week. As for the old one, there on the left, it looked as dead as ever; or else the so-called buds were so brown they did not show up from this distance. Perhaps the shedding of the branch had been its finish. And a good job too.

He turned away from the window and set about rearranging the room to his taste, spreading his things about. He liked pottering, opening drawers, taking things out and putting them back again. There was a red pencil in one of the side tables that must have slipped down behind a pile of books and been found during the turn-out. He sharpened it, gave it a sleek fine point. He found a new film in another drawer, and kept it out to put in his camera in the morning. There were a number of papers and old photographs in the drawer, heaped in a jumble, and snapshots too, dozens of them. Midge used to look after these things at one time and put them in albums; then during the war she must have lost interest, or had too many other things to do.

All this junk could really be cleared away. It would have made a fine fire the other night, and might have got even the apple logs to burn. There was little sense in keeping any of it. This appalling photo of Midge, for instance, taken heaven knows how many years ago, not long after their marriage, judging from the style of it. Did she really wear her hair that way? That fluffy mop, much too thick and bushy for her face, which was long and narrow even then. The low neck, pointing to a V, and the dangling earrings, and the smile, too eager, making her mouth seem larger than it was. In the left hand corner she had written 'To my own darling Buzz, from his loving Midge.' He had completely forgotten his old nickname. It had been dropped years back, and he seemed to remember he had never cared for it: he had found it ridiculous and embarrassing and had chided her for using it in front of people.

He tore the photograph in half and threw it on the fire. He watched it curl up upon itself and burn, and the last to go was that vivid smile. My own darling Buzz . . . Suddenly he remembered the evening dress in the photograph. It was green, not her colour ever, turning her sallow; and she had bought it for some special occasion, some big dinner party with friends who were celebrating their wedding anniversary. The idea of the dinner had been to invite all those friends and neighbours who had been married roughly around the same time, which was the reason Midge and he had gone.

There was a lot of champagne, and one or two speeches, and much conviviality, laughter, and joking—some of the joking rather broad—and he remembered that when the evening was over, and they were climbing into the car to drive away, his host, with a gust of laughter, said, 'Try paying your addresses in a top hat, old boy, they say it never fails!' He had been aware of Midge beside him, in that green evening frock, sitting very straight and still, and on her face that same smile which she had worn in the photograph just destroyed, eager yet uncertain, doubtful of the meaning of the words that her host, slightly intoxicated, had let fall upon the evening air, yet wishing to seem advanced, anxious to please, and more than either of these things desperately anxious to attract.

When he had put the car away in the garage and gone into the house he had found her waiting there, in the living room, for no reason at all. Her coat was thrown off to show the evening dress, and the smile, rather uncertain, was on her face.

He yawned, and settling himself down in a chair picked up a book. She waited a little while, then slowly took up her coat and went upstairs. It must have been shortly afterwards that she had that photograph taken. 'My own darling Buzz, from his loving Midge.' He threw a great handful of dry sticks on to the fire. They crackled and split and turned the photograph to ashes. No damp green logs tonight . . .

It was fine and warm the following day. The sun shone, and the birds sang. He had a sudden impulse to go to London. It was a day for sauntering along Bond Street, watching the passing crowds. A day for calling in at his tailors, for having a haircut, for eating a dozen oysters at his favourite bar. The chill had left him. The pleasant hours stretched before him. He might even look in at a matinée.

The day passed without incident, peaceful, untiring, just as he had planned, making a change from day-by-day country routine. He drove home about seven o'clock, looking forward to his drink and to his dinner. It was so warm he did not need his overcoat, not even now, with the sun gone down. He waved a hand to the farmer, who happened to be passing the gate as he turned into the drive.

'Lovely day,' he shouted.

The man nodded, smiled. 'Can do with plenty of these from now on,' he shouted back. Decent fellow. They had always been very matey since those war days, when he had driven the tractor. He put away the car and had a drink, and while waiting for supper took a stroll around the garden. What a difference those hours of sunshine had made to everything. Several daffodils were out, narcissi too, and the green hedgerows fresh and sprouting. As for the apple trees, the buds had burst, and they were all of them in flower. He went to his little favourite and touched the blossom. It felt soft to his hand and he gently shook a bough. It was firm, well-set, and would not fall. The scent was scarcely perceptible as yet, but in a day or two, with a little more sun, perhaps a shower or two, it would come from the open flower and softly fill the air, never pungent, never strong, a modest scent. A scent which you would have to find for yourself, as the bees did. Once found it stayed with you, it lingered always, alluring, comforting, and sweet. He patted the little tree, and went down the steps into the house.

Next morning, at breakfast, there came a knock on the dining-room window, and the daily woman said that Willis was outside and wanted to have a word with him. He asked Willis to step in.

The gardener looked aggrieved. Was it trouble, then?

'I'm sorry to bother you, sir,' he said, 'but I had a few words with Mr. Jackson this morning. He's been complaining.'

Jackson was the farmer, who owned the neighbouring fields. 'What's he complaining about?'

'Says I've been throwing wood over the fence into his field, and the young foal out there, with the mare, tripped over it and went lame. I've never thrown wood over the fence in my life, sir. Quite nasty he was, sir. Spoke of the value of the foal, and it might spoil his chances to sell it.'

'I hope you told him, then, it wasn't true.'

'I did, sir. But the point is someone has been throwing wood over the fence. He showed me the very spot. Just behind the garage. I went with Mr. Jackson, and there they were. Logs had been tipped there, sir. I thought it best to come to you about it before I spoke in the kitchen, otherwise you know how it is, there would be unpleasantness.'

He felt the gardener's eye upon him. No way out, of course.

And it was Willis's fault in the first place.

'No need to say anything in the kitchen, Willis,' he said. 'I threw the logs there myself. You brought them into the house, without my asking you to do so, with the result that they put out my fire, filled the room with smoke, and ruined an evening. I chucked them over the fence in a devil of a temper, and if they have damaged Jackson's foal you can apologize for me, and tell him I'll pay him compensation. All I ask is that you don't bring any more logs like those into the house again.'

'No sir, I understood they had not been a success. I didn't think, though, that you would go so far as to throw them out.'

'Well, I did. And there's an end to it.'

'Yes, sir.' He made as if to go, but before he left the dining room he paused and said, 'I can't understand about the logs not burning, all the same. I took a small piece back to the wife, and it burnt lovely in our kitchen, bright as anything.'

'It did not burn here.'

'Anyway, the old tree is making up for one spoilt branch, sir. Have you seen her this morning?'

'No.'

'It's yesterday's sun that has done it, sir, and the warm night. Quite a treat she is, with all the blossom. You should go out and take a look at her directly.'

Willis left the room, and he continued his breakfast.

Presently he went out on to the terrace. At first he did not go up on to the lawn; he made a pretence of seeing to other things, of getting the heavy garden seat out, now that the weather was set fair. And then, fetching a pair of clippers, he did a bit of pruning to the few roses, under the windows. Yet, finally, something drew him to the tree.

It was just as Willis said. Whether it was the sun, the warmth, the mild still night, he could not tell; but the small brown buds had unfolded themselves, had ripened into flower, and now spread themselves above his head into a fantastic cloud of white, moist blossom. It grew thickest at the top of the tree, the flowers so clustered together that they looked like wad upon wad of soggy cotton wool, and all of it, from the topmost branches to those

nearer to the ground, had this same pallid colour of sickly white.

It did not resemble a tree at all; it might have been a flapping tent, left out in the rain by campers who had gone away, or else a mop, a giant mop, whose streaky surface had been caught somehow by the sun, and so turned bleached. The blossom was too thick, too great a burden for the long thin trunk, and the moisture clinging to it made it heavier still. Already, as if the effort had been too much, the lower flowers, those nearest the ground, were turning brown; yet there had been no rain.

Well, there it was. Willis had been proved right. The tree had blossomed. But instead of blossoming to life, to beauty, it had somehow, deep in nature, gone awry and turned a freak. A freak which did not know its texture or its shape, but thought to please. Almost as though it said, self-conscious, with a smirk, 'Look. All this is for you.'

Suddenly he heard a step behind him. It was Willis. 'Fine sight, sir, isn't it?'

'Sorry, I don't admire it. The blossom is far too thick.'

The gardener stared at him and said nothing. It struck him that Willis must think him very difficult, very hard, and possibly eccentric. He would go and discuss him in the kitchen with the daily woman.

He forced himself to smile at Willis.

'Look here,' he said, 'I don't mean to damp you. But all this blossom doesn't interest me. I prefer it small and light and colourful, like the little tree. But you take some of it back home, to your wife. Cut as much of it as you like, I don't mind at all. I'd like you to have it.'

He waved his arm, generously. He wanted Willis to go now, and fetch a ladder, and carry the stuff away.

The man shook his head. He looked quite shocked.

'No, thank you, sir, I wouldn't dream of it. It would spoil the tree. I want to wait for the fruit. That's what I'm banking on, the fruit.'

There was no more to be said.

'All right, Willis. Don't bother, then.'

He went back to the terrace. But when he sat down there in the sun, looking up the sloping lawn, he could not see the little tree at all, standing modest and demure above the steps, her soft flowers lifting to the sky. She was dwarfed and hidden by the freak, with its great cloud of sagging petals, already wilting, dingy white, on to the grass beneath. And whichever way he turned his chair, this way or that upon the terrace, it seemed to him that he could not escape the tree, that it stood there above him, reproachful, anxious, desirous of the admiration that he could not give.

That summer he took a longer holiday than he had done for many years—a bare ten days with his old mother in Norfolk, instead of the customary month that he had been used to spend with Midge, and the rest of August and the whole of September in Switzerland and Italy.

He took his car, and so was free to motor from place to place as the mood inclined. He cared little for sightseeing or excursions, and was not much of a climber. What he liked most was to come upon a little town in the cool of the evening, pick out a small but comfortable hotel, and then stay there, if it pleased him, for two or three days at a time, doing nothing, mooching.

He liked sitting about in the sun all morning, at some café or restaurant, with a glass of wine in front of him, watching the people; so many gay young creatures seemed to travel nowadays. He enjoyed the chatter of conversation around him, as long as he did not have to join in; and now and again a smile would come his way, a word or two of greeting from some guest in the same hotel, but nothing to commit him, merely a sense of being in the swim, of being a man of leisure on his own, abroad.

The difficulty in the old days, on holiday anywhere with Midge, would be her habit of striking up acquaintance with people, some other couple who struck her as looking 'nice' or, as she put it, 'our sort.' It would start with conversation over coffee, and then pass on to mutual planning of shared days, car drives in foursomes—he could not bear it, the holiday would be ruined.

Now, thank heaven, there was no need for this. He did what he liked, in his own time. There was no Midge to say, 'Well, shall we be moving?' when he was still sitting contentedly over his wine, no Midge to plan a visit to some old church that did not interest him.

He put on weight during his holiday, and he did not mind. There was no one to suggest a good long walk to keep fit after the rich food, thus spoiling the pleasant somnolence that comes with coffee and dessert; no one to glance, surprised, at the sudden wearing of a jaunty shirt, a flamboyant tie.

Strolling through the little towns and villages, hatless, smoking a cigar, receiving smiles from the jolly young folk around him, he felt himself a dog. This was the life, no worries, no cares. No 'We have to be back on the fifteenth because of that committee meeting at the hospital'; no 'We can't possibly leave the house shut up for longer than a fortnight, something might happen.' Instead, the bright lights of a little country fair, in a village whose name he did not even bother to find out; the tinkle of music, boys and girls laughing, and he himself, after a bottle of the local wine, bowing to a young thing with a gay handkerchief round her head and sweeping her off to dance under the hot tent. No matter if her steps did not harmonize with his—it was years since he had danced—this was the thing, this was it. He released her when the music stopped, and off she ran, giggling, back to her young friends, laughing at him no doubt. What of it? He had had his fun.

He left Italy when the weather turned, at the end of September, and was back home the first week in October. No problem to it. A telegram to the daily woman, with the probable date of arrival, and that was all. Even a brief holiday with Midge and the return meant complications. Written instructions about groceries, milk, and bread; airing of beds, lighting of fires, reminders about the delivery of the morning papers. The whole business turned into a chore.

He turned into the drive on a mellow October evening and there was smoke coming from the chimneys, the front door open, and his pleasant home awaiting him. No rushing through to the back regions to learn of possible plumbing disasters, breakages, water shortages, food difficulties; the daily woman knew better than to bother him with these. Merely, 'Good evening, sir. I hope you had a good holiday. Supper at the usual time?' And then silence. He could have his drink, light his pipe, and relax; the small pile of letters did not matter. No feverish tearing of them open, and then the start of the telephoning, the hearing of those endless one-sided conversations between women friends. 'Well? How are things? Really? My dear ... And what did you say to that? ... She did? ... I can't possibly on Wednesday ...'

He stretched himself contentedly, stiff after his drive, and gazed comfortably around the cheerful, empty living room. He was hungry, after his journey up from Dover, and the chop seemed rather meagre after foreign fare. But there it was, it wouldn't hurt him to return to plainer food. A sardine on toast followed the chop, and then he looked about him for dessert.

There was a plate of apples on the sideboard. He fetched them and put them down in front of him on the dining-room table. Poor looking things. Small and wizened, dullish brown in colour. He bit into one, but as soon as the taste of it was on his tongue he spat it out. The thing was rotten. He tried another. It was just the same. He looked more closely at the pile of apples. The skins were leathery and rough and hard; you would expect the insides to be sour. On the contrary they were pulpy soft, and the cores were yellow. Filthy-tasting things. A stray piece stuck to his tooth and he pulled it out. Stringy, beastly . . .

He rang the bell, and the woman came through from the kitchen.

'Have we any other dessert?' he said.

'I am afraid not, sir. I remembered how fond you were of apples, and Willis brought in these from the garden. He said they were especially good, and just ripe for eating.'

'Well, he's quite wrong. They're uneatable.'

'I'm very sorry, sir. I wouldn't have put them through had I known. There's a lot more outside, too. Willis brought in a great basketful.'

'All the same sort?'

'Yes, sir. The small brown ones. No other kind, at all.'

'Never mind, it can't be helped. I'll look for myself in the morning.'

He got up from the table and went through to the living room.

He had a glass of port to take away the taste of the apples, but it seemed to make no difference, not even a biscuit with it. The pulpy rotten tang clung to his tongue and the roof of his mouth, and in the end he was obliged to go up to the bathroom and clean his teeth. The maddening thing was that he could have done with a good clean apple, after that rather indifferent supper: something with a smooth clear skin, the inside not too sweet, a little sharp in flavour. He knew the kind. Good biting texture. You had to pick them, of course, at just the right moment.

He dreamt that night he was back again in Italy, dancing under the tent in the little cobbled square. He woke with the tinkling music in his ear, but he could not recall the face of the peasant girl or remember the feel of her, tripping against his feet. He tried to recapture the memory, lying awake, over his morning tea, but it eluded him.

He got up out of bed and went over to the window, to glance at the weather. Fine enough, with a slight nip in the air.

Then he saw the tree. The sight of it came as a shock, it was so unexpected. Now he realized at once where the apples had come from the night before. The tree was laden, bowed down, under her burden of fruit. They clustered, small and brown, on every branch, diminishing in size as they reached the top, so that those on the high boughs, not grown yet to full size, looked like nuts. They weighed heavy on the tree, and because of this it seemed bent and twisted out of shape, the lower branches nearly sweeping the ground; and on the grass, at the foot of the tree, were more and yet more apples, windfalls, the first-grown, pushed off by their clamouring brothers and sisters. The ground was covered with them, many split open and rotting where the wasps had been. Never in his life had he seen a tree so laden with fruit. It was a miracle that it had not fallen under the weight.

He went out before breakfast—curiosity was too great—and stood beside the tree, staring at it. There was no mistake about it, these were the same apples that had been put in the dining room last night. Hardly bigger than tangerines, and many of them smaller than that, they grew so close together on the branches that to pick one you would be forced to pick a dozen.

There was something monstrous in the sight, something distasteful; yet it was pitiful too that the months had brought this agony upon the tree, for agony it was, there could be no other word for it. The tree was tortured by fruit, groaning under the weight of it, and the frightful part about it was that not one of the fruit was eatable. Every apple was rotten through and through. He trod them underfoot, the windfalls on the grass, there was no escaping them; and in a moment they were mush and slime, clinging about his heels—he had to clean the mess off with wisps of grass.

It would have been far better if the tree had died, stark and bare, before this ever happened. What use was it to him or anyone, this load of rotting fruit, littering up the place, fouling the ground? And the tree itself humped, as it were, in pain, and yet he could almost swear triumphant, gloating.

Just as in spring, when the mass of fluffy blossom, colourless and sodden, dragged the reluctant eye away from the other trees, so it did now. Impossible to avoid seeing the tree, with its burden of fruit. Every window in the front part of the house looked out upon it. And he knew how it would be. The fruit would cling there until it was picked, staying upon the branches through October and November, and it never would be picked, because nobody could eat it. He could see himself being bothered with the tree throughout the autumn. Whenever he came out on to the terrace there it would be, sagging and loathsome.

It was extraordinary the dislike he had taken to the tree. It was a perpetual reminder of the fact that he ... well, he was blessed if he knew what ... a perpetual reminder of all the things he most detested, and always had, he could not put a name to them. He decided then and there that Willis should pick the fruit and take it away, sell it, get rid of it, anything, as long as he did not have to eat it, and as long as he was not forced to watch the tree drooping there, day after day, throughout the autumn.

He turned his back upon it and was relieved to see that none of the other trees had so degraded themselves to excess. They carried a fair crop, nothing out of the way, and as he might have known the young tree, to the right of the old one, made a brave little show on its own, with a light load of medium-sized, rosy-looking apples, not too dark in colour, but freshly reddened where the sun had ripened them. He would pick one now, and take it in, to eat with breakfast. He made his choice, and the apple fell at the first touch into his hand. It looked so good that he bit into it with appetite. That was it, juicy, sweet-smelling, sharp, the dew upon it still. He did not look back at the old tree. He went indoors, hungry, to breakfast.

It took the gardener nearly a week to strip the tree, and it was plain he did it under protest.

'I don't care what you do with them,' said his employer. 'You can sell them and keep the money, or you can take them home and feed them to your pigs. I can't stand the sight of them, and that's all there is to it. Find a long ladder, and start on the job right away.'

It seemed to him that Willis, from sheer obstinacy, spun out the time. He would watch the man from the windows act as though in slow motion. First the placing of the ladder. Then the laborious climb, and the descent to steady it again. After that the performance of plucking off the fruit, dropping them, one by one, into the basket. Day after day it was the same. Willis was always there on the sloping lawn with his ladder, under the tree, the branches creaking and groaning, and beneath him on the grass baskets, pails, basins, any receptacle that would hold the apples.

At last the job was finished. The ladder was removed, the baskets and pails also, and the tree was stripped bare. He looked out at it, the evening of that day, in satisfaction. No more rotting fruit to offend his eye. Every single apple gone.

Yet the tree, instead of seeming lighter from the loss of its burden, looked, if it were possible, more dejected than ever. The branches still sagged, and the leaves, withering now to the cold autumnal evening, folded upon themselves and shivered. 'Is this my reward?' it seemed to say. 'After all I've done for you?'

As the light faded, the shadow of the tree cast a blight upon the dank night. Winter would soon come. And the short, dull days.

He had never cared much for the fall of the year. In the old days, when he went up to London every day to the office, it had meant that early start by train, on a nippy morning. And then, before three o'clock in the afternoon, the clerks were turning on the lights, and as often as not there would be fog in the air, murky and dismal, and a slow chugging journey home, daily bread-ers like himself sitting five abreast in a carriage, some of them with colds in their heads. Then the long evening followed, with Midge opposite him before the living room fire, and he listening, or feigning to listen, to the account of her days and the things that had gone wrong.

If she had not shouldered any actual household disaster, she would pick upon some current event to cast a gloom. 'I see fares are going up again, what about your season ticket?,' or 'This business in South Africa looks nasty, quite a long bit about it on the six o'clock news,' or yet again 'Three more cases of polio over at the isolation hospital. I don't know, I'm sure, what the medical world thinks it's doing . . .'

Now, at least, he was spared the role of listener, but the memory of those long evenings was with him still, and when the lights were lit and the curtains were drawn he would be reminded of the click-click of the needles, the aimless chatter, and the 'Heigh-ho' of the yawns. He began to drop in, sometimes before supper, sometimes afterwards, at the Green Man, the old public house a quarter of a mile away on the main road. Nobody bothered him there. He would sit in a corner, having said good evening to genial Mrs. Hill, the proprietress, and then, with a cigarette and a whisky-and-soda, watch the local inhabitants stroll in to have a pint, to throw a dart, to gossip.

In a sense it made a continuation of his summer holiday. It bore resemblance, admittedly slight, to the carefree atmosphere of the cafés and the restaurants; and there was a kind of warmth about the bright smoke-filled bar, crowded with working men who did not bother him, which he found pleasant, comforting.

These visits cut into the length of the dark winter evenings, making them more tolerable.

A cold in the head, caught in mid-December, put a stop to this for more than a week. He was obliged to keep to the house. And it was odd, he thought to himself, how much he missed the Green Man, and how sick to death he became of sitting about in the living room or in the study, with nothing to do but read or listen to the wireless. The cold and the boredom made him morose and irritable, and the enforced inactivity turned his liver sluggish. He needed exercise. Whatever the weather, he decided towards the end of yet another cold grim day, he would go out tomorrow. The sky had been heavy from mid-afternoon and threatened snow, but no matter, he could not stand the house for a further twenty-four hours without a break.

The final edge to his irritation came with the fruit tart at supper. He was in that

final stage of a bad cold when the taste is not yet fully returned, appetite is poor, but there is a certain emptiness within that needs ministration of a particular kind. A bird might have done it. Half a partridge, roasted to perfection, followed by a cheese soufflé. As well ask for the moon. The daily woman, not gifted with imagination, produced plaice, of all fish the most tasteless, the most dry. When she had borne the remains of this away—he had left most of it upon his plate—she returned with a tart, and because hunger was far from being satisfied he helped himself to it liberally.

One taste was enough. Choking, spluttering, he spat out the contents of his spoon upon the plate. He got up and rang the bell.

The woman appeared, a query on her face, at the unexpected summons.

'What the devil is this stuff?'

'Jam tart, sir.'

'What sort of jam?'

'Apple jam, sir. Made from my own bottling.'

He threw down his napkin on the table.

'I guessed as much. You've been using some of those apples that I complained to you about months ago. I told you and Willis quite distinctly that I would not have any of those apples in the house.'

The woman's face became tight and drawn.

'You said, sir, not to cook the apples, or to bring them in for dessert. You said nothing about not making jam. I thought they would taste all right as jam. And I made some myself, to try. It was perfectly all right. So I made several bottles of jam from the apples Willis gave me. We always made jam here, madam and myself.'

'Well, I'm sorry for your trouble, but I can't eat it. Those apples disagreed with me in the autumn, and whether they are made into jam or whatever you like they will do so again. Take the tart away, and don't let me see it, or the jam, again. I'll have some coffee in the living room.'

He went out of the room, trembling. It was fantastic that such a small incident should make him feel so angry. God! What fools people were. She knew, Willis knew, that he disliked the apples, loathed the taste and smell of them, but in their cheese-paring way they decided that it would save money if he was given homemade jam, jam made from the apples he particularly detested.

He swallowed down a stiff whisky and lit a cigarette.

In a moment or two she appeared with the coffee. She did not retire immediately on putting down the tray.

'Could I have a word with you, sir?'

'What is it?'

'I think it would be for the best if I gave in my notice.'

Now this, on top of the other. What a day, what an evening.

'What reason? Because I can't eat apple tart?'

'It's not just that, sir. Somehow I feel things are very different from what they were. I have meant to speak several times.'

'I don't give much trouble, do I?'

'No, sir. Only in the old days, when madam was alive, I felt my work was appreciated. Now it's as though it didn't matter one way or the other. Nothing's ever said, and although I try to do my best I can't be sure. I think I'd be happier if I went where there was a lady again who took notice of what I did.'

'You are the best judge of that, of course. I'm sorry if you haven't liked it here lately.'

'You were away so much too, sir, this summer. When madam was alive it was never for more than a fortnight. Everything seems so changed. I don't know where I am, or Willis either.'

'So Willis is fed up too?'

'That's not for me to say, of course. I know he was upset about the apples, but that's some time ago. Perhaps he'll be speaking to you himself.'

'Perhaps he will. I had no idea I was causing so much concern to you both. All right, that's quite enough. Goodnight.'

She went out of the room. He stared moodily about him. Good riddance to them both, if that was how they felt. Things aren't the same. Everything so changed. Damned nonsense. As for Willis being upset about the apples, what infernal impudence. Hadn't he a right to do what he liked with his own tree? To hell with his cold and with the weather. He couldn't bear sitting about in front of the fire thinking about Willis and the cook. He would go down to the Green Man and forget the whole thing. He put on his overcoat and muffler and his old cap and walked briskly down the road, and in twenty minutes he was sitting in his usual corner in the Green Man, with Mrs. Hill pouring out his whisky and expressing her delight to see him back. One or two of the habitués smiled at him, asked after his health. 'Had a cold, sir? Same everywhere. Everyone's got one.'

'That's right.'

'Well, it's the time of year, isn't it?'

'Got to expect it. It's when it's on the chest it's nasty.'

'No worse than being stuffed up, like, in the head.'

'That's right. One's as bad as the other. Nothing to it.'

Likeable fellows. Friendly. Not harping at one, not bothering.

'Another whisky, please.'

'There you are, sir. Do you good. Keep out the cold.'

Mrs. Hill beamed behind the bar. Large, comfortable old soul. Through a haze of smoke he heard the chatter, the deep laughter, the click of the darts, the jocular roar at a bull's eye.

'. . . and if it comes on to snow, I don't know how we shall manage,' Mrs. Hill was saying, 'them being so late delivering the coal. If we had a load of logs it would help us out, but what do you think they're asking? Two pounds a load. I mean to say . . .'

He leant forward and his voice sounded far away, even to himself.

'I'll let you have some logs,' he said.

Mrs. Hill turned round. She had not been talking to him.

'Excuse me?' she said.

'I'll let you have some logs,' he repeated. 'Got an old tree, up at home, needed sawing down for months. Do it for you tomorrow.'

He nodded, smiling.

'Oh no, sir. I couldn't think of putting you to the trouble. The coal will turn up, never fear.'

'No trouble at all. A pleasure. Like to do it for you, the exercise, you know, do me good. Putting on weight. You count on me.'

He got down from his seat and reached, rather carefully, for his coat.

'It's apple wood,' he said. 'Do you mind apple wood?'

'Why no,' she answered, 'any wood will do. But can you spare it, sir?'

He nodded, mysteriously. It was a bargain, it was a secret.

'I'll bring it down to you in my trailer tomorrow night,' he said.

'Careful, sir,' she said, 'mind the step...'

He walked home, through the cold crisp night, smiling to himself. He did not remember undressing or getting into bed, but when he woke the next morning the first thought that came to his mind was the promise he had made about the tree.

It was not one of Willis's days, he realized with satisfaction. There would be no interfering with his plan. The sky was heavy and snow had fallen in the night. More to come. But as yet nothing to worry about, nothing to hamper him.

He went through to the kitchen garden, after breakfast, to the tool shed. He took down the saw, the wedges, and the axe. He might need all of them. He ran his thumb along the edges. They would do. As he shouldered his tools and walked back to the front garden he laughed to himself, thinking that he must resemble an executioner of old days, setting forth to behead some wretched victim in the Tower.

He laid his tools down beneath the apple tree. It would be an act of mercy, really. Never had he seen anything so wretched, so utterly woebegone, as the apple tree. There couldn't be any life left in it. Not a leaf remained. Twisted, ugly, bent, it ruined the appearance of the lawn. Once it was out of the way the whole setting of the garden would change.

A snowflake fell on to his hand, then another. He glanced down past the terrace to the dining-room window. He could see the woman laying his lunch. He went down the steps and into the house. 'Look,' he said, 'if you like to leave my lunch ready in the oven, I think I'll fend for myself today. I may be busy, and I don't want to be pinned down for time. Also it's going to snow. You had better go off early today and get home, in case it becomes really bad. I can manage perfectly well. And I prefer it.'

Perhaps she thought his decision came through offence at her giving notice the night before. Whatever she thought, he did not mind. He wanted to be alone. He wanted no face peering from the window.

She went off at about twelve-thirty, and as soon as she had gone he went to the oven and got his lunch. He meant to get it over, so that he could give up the whole short afternoon to the felling of the tree.

No more snow had fallen, apart from a few flakes that did not lie. He took off his coat, rolled up his sleeves, and seized the saw. With his left hand he ripped away the wire at the base of the tree. Then he placed the saw about a foot from the bottom and began to work it, backwards, forwards.

For the first dozen strokes all went smoothly. The saw bit into the wood, the teeth took hold. Then after a few moments the saw began to bind. He had been afraid of that.

He tried to work it free, but the opening that he had made was not yet large enough, and the tree gripped upon the saw and held it fast. He drove in the first wedge, with no result. He drove in the second, and the opening gaped a little wider, but still not wide enough to release the saw.

He pulled and tugged at the saw, to no avail. He began to lose his temper. He took up his axe and started hacking at the tree, pieces of the trunk flying outwards, scattering on the grass.

That was more like it. That was the answer.

Up and down went the heavy axe, splitting and tearing at the tree. Off came the peeling bark, the great white strips of underwood, raw and stringy. Hack at it, blast at it, gouge at the tough tissue, throw the axe away, claw at the rubbery flesh with the bare hands. Not far enough yet, go on, go on.

There goes the saw, the wedge, released. Now up with the axe again. Down there, heavy, where the stringy threads cling so steadfast. Now she's groaning, now she's splitting, now she's rocking and swaying, hanging there upon one bleeding strip. Boot her, then. That's it, kick her, kick her again, one final blow, she's over, she's falling . . . she's down . . . damn her, blast her . . . she's down, splitting the air with sound, and all her branches spread about her on the ground.

He stood back, wiping the sweat from his forehead, from his chin. The wreckage surrounded him on either side, and below him, at his feet, gaped the torn, white, jagged stump of the axed tree.

It began snowing.

His first task, after felling the apple tree, was to hack off the branches and the smaller boughs, and so to grade the wood in stacks, which made it easier to drag away.

The small stuff, bundled and roped, would do for kindling; Mrs. Hill would no doubt be glad of that as well. He brought the car, with the trailer attached, to the garden gate, hard by the terrace. This chopping up of the branches was simple work; much of it could be done with a hook. The fatigue came with bending and tying the bundles, and then heaving them down past the terrace and through the gate up on to the trailer. The thicker branches he disposed of with the axe, then split them into three or four lengths, which he could also rope and drag, one by one, to the trailer.

He was fighting all the while against time. The light, what there was of it, would be gone by half past four, and the snow went on falling. The ground was already covered, and when he paused for a moment in his work, and wiped the sweat away from his face, the thin frozen flakes fell upon his lips and made their way, insidious and soft, down his collar to his neck and body. If he lifted his eyes to the sky he was blinded at once. The flakes came thicker, faster, swirling about his head, and it was as though the heaven had turned itself into a canopy of snow, ever descending, coming nearer, closer, stifling the earth. The snow fell upon the torn boughs and the hacked branches, hampering his work. If he rested but an instant to draw breath and renew his strength, it seemed to throw a protective cover, soft and white, over the pile of wood.

He could not wear gloves. If he did so he had no grip upon his hook or his axe, nor could he tie the rope and drag the branches. His fingers were numb with cold, soon they would be too stiff to bend. He had a pain now, under the heart, from the strain of dragging the stuff on to the trailer; and the work never seemed to lessen. Whenever he returned to the fallen tree the pile of wood would appear as high as ever, long boughs, short boughs, a heap of kindling there, nearly covered with the snow, which he had forgotten: all must be roped and fastened and carried or pulled away.

It was after half past four, and almost dark, when he had disposed of all the branches, and nothing now remained but to drag the trunk, already hacked into three lengths, over the terrace to the waiting trailer.

He was very nearly at the point of exhaustion. Only his will to be rid of the tree kept him to the task. His breath came slowly, painfully, and all the while the snow fell into his mouth and into his eyes and he could barely see.

He took his rope and slid it under the cold slippery trunk, knotting it fiercely. How hard and unyielding was the naked wood, and the bark was rough, hurting his numb hands.

'That's the end of you,' he muttered, 'that's your finish.'

Staggering to his feet he bore the weight of the heavy trunk over his shoulder, and began to drag it slowly down over the slope to the terrace and to the garden gate. It followed him, bump . . . bump . . . down the steps of the terrace. Heavy and lifeless, the last bare limbs of the apple tree dragged in his wake through the wet snow.

It was over. His task was done. He stood panting, one hand upon the trailer. Now nothing more remained but to take the stuff down to the Green Man before the snow made the drive impossible. He had chains for the car, he had thought of that already.

He went into the house to change the clothes that were clinging to him and to have a drink. Never mind about his fire, never mind about drawing curtains, seeing what there might be for supper, all the chores the daily woman usually did—that would come later. He must have his drink and get the wood away.

His mind was numb and weary, like his hands and his whole body. For a moment he thought of leaving the job until the following day, flopping down into the arm-chair, and closing his eyes. No, it would not do. Tomorrow there would be more snow, tomorrow the drive would be two or three feet deep. He knew the signs. And there would be the trailer, stuck outside the garden gate, with the pile of wood inside it, frozen white. He must make the effort and do the job tonight.

He finished his drink, changed, and went out to start the car. It was still snowing, but now that darkness had fallen a colder, cleaner feeling had come into the air, and it was freezing. The dizzy, swirling flakes came more slowly now, with precision.

The engine started and he began to drive downhill, the trailer in tow. He drove slowly, and very carefully, because of the heavy load. And it was an added strain, after the hard work of the afternoon, peering through the falling snow, wiping the windscreen. Never had the lights of the Green Man shone more cheerfully as he pulled up into the little yard.

He blinked as he stood within the doorway, smiling to himself. 'Well, I've brought your wood,' he said.

Mrs. Hill stared at him from behind the bar, one or two fellows turned and looked at him, and a hush fell upon the dart-players. 'You never ...' began Mrs. Hill, but he jerked his head at the door and laughed at her.

'Go and see,' he said, 'but don't ask me to unload it tonight.'

He moved to his favourite corner, chuckling to himself, and there they all were, exclaiming and talking and laughing by the door, and he was quite a hero, the fellows crowding round with questions, and Mrs. Hill pouring out his whisky and thanking him and laughing and shaking her head. 'You'll drink on the house tonight,' she said.

'Not a bit of it,' he said, 'this is my party. Rounds one and two to me. Come on, you chaps.'

It was festive, warm, jolly, and good luck to them all, he kept saying, good luck to Mrs. Hill, and to himself, and to the whole world. When was Christmas? Next week, the week after? Well, here's to it, and a merry

Christmas. Never mind the snow, never mind the weather. For the first time he was one of them, not isolated in his corner. For the first time he drank with them, he laughed with them, he even threw a dart with them, and there they all were in that warm stuffy smoke-filled bar, and he felt they liked him, he belonged, he was no longer 'the gentleman' from the house up the road.

The hours passed, and some of them went home, and others took their place, and he was still sitting there, hazy, comfortable, the warmth and the smoke blending together. Nothing of what he heard or saw made very much sense but somehow it did not seem to matter, for there was jolly, fat, easy-going Mrs. Hill to minister to his needs, her face glowing at him over the bar.

Another face swung into his view, that of one of the labourers from the farm, with whom, in the old war days, he had shared the driving of the tractor. He leant forward, touching the fellow on the shoulder.

'What happened to the little girl?' he said.

The man lowered his tankard. 'Beg pardon, sir?' he said.

'You remember. The little land girl. She used to milk the cows, feed the pigs, up at the farm. Pretty girl, dark curly hair, always smiling.'

Mrs. Hill turned round from serving another customer.

'Does the gentleman mean May, I wonder?' she asked.

'Yes, that's it, that was the name, young May,' he said.

'Why, didn't you ever hear about it, sir?' said Mrs. Hill, filling up his glass. 'We were all very much shocked at the time, everyone was talking of it, weren't they, Fred?'

'That's right, Mrs. Hill.'

The man wiped his mouth with the back of his hand.

'Killed,' he said, 'thrown from the back of some chap's motorbike. Going to be married very shortly. About four years ago, now. Dreadful thing, eh? Nice kid too.'

'We all sent a wreath, from just around,' said Mrs. Hill. 'Her mother wrote back, very touched, and sent a cutting from the local paper, didn't she, Fred? Quite a big funeral they had, ever so many floral tributes. Poor May. We were all fond of May.'

'That's right,' said Fred.

'And fancy you never hearing about it, sir!' said Mrs. Hill.

'No,' he said, 'no, nobody ever told me. I'm sorry about it. Very sorry.'

He stared in front of him at his half-filled glass.

The conversation went on around him but he was no longer part of the company. He was on his own again, silent, in his corner. Dead. That poor, pretty girl was dead. Thrown off a motorbike. Been dead for three or four years. Some careless, bloody fellow, taking a corner too fast, the girl behind him, clinging on to his belt, laughing probably in his ear, and then crash . . . finish. No more curling hair, blowing about her face, no more laughter. May, that was the name; he remembered clearly now. He could see her smiling over her shoulder, when they called to her. 'Coming,' she sang out, and put a clattering pail down in the yard and went off, whistling, with big clumping boots. He had put his arm about her and kissed her for one brief, fleeting moment. May, the land girl, with the laughing eyes.

'Going, sir?' said Mrs. Hill.

'Yes. Yes, I think I'll be going now.'

He stumbled to the entrance and opened the door. It had frozen hard during the past hour and it was no longer snowing. The heavy pall had gone from the sky and the stars shone.

'Want a hand with the car, sir?' said someone.

'No, thank you,' he said, 'I can manage.'

He unhitched the trailer and let it fall. Some of the wood lurched forward heavily. That would do tomorrow. Tomorrow, if he felt like it, he would come down again and help to unload the wood. Not tonight. He had done enough. Now he was really tired; now he was spent.

It took him some time to start the car, and before he was halfway up the side-road leading to his house he realized that he had made a mistake to bring it at all. The snow was heavy all about him, and the track he had made earlier in the evening was now covered. The car lurched and slithered, and suddenly the right wheel dipped and the whole body plunged sideways. He had got into a drift.

He climbed out and looked about him. The car was deep in the drift, impossible to move without two or three men to help him, and even then, if he went for assistance, what hope was there of trying to continue further, with the snow just as thick ahead? Better leave it. Try again in the morning, when he was fresh. No sense in hanging about now, spending half the night pushing and shoving at the car, all to no purpose. No harm would come to it, here on the side road; nobody else would be coming this way tonight.

He started walking up the road towards his own drive. It was bad luck that he had got the car into the drift. In the centre of the road the going was not bad and the snow did not come above his ankles. He thrust his hands deep in the pockets of his overcoat and ploughed on, up the hill, the countryside a great white waste on either side of him.

He remembered that he had sent the daily woman home at midday and that the house would strike cheerless and cold on his return. The fire would have gone out, and in all probability the furnace too. The windows, uncurtained, would stare bleakly down at him, letting in the night. Supper to get into the bargain. Well, it was his own fault. No one to blame but himself. This was the moment when there should be someone waiting, someone to come running through from the living room to the hall, opening the

front door, flooding the hall with light. 'Are you all right, darling? I was getting anxious.'

He paused for breath at the top of the hill and saw his home, shrouded by trees, at the end of the short drive. It looked dark and forbidding, without a light in any window. There was more friendliness in the open, under the bright stars, standing on the crisp white snow, than in the sombre house.

He had left the side gate open, and he went through that way to the terrace, shutting the gate behind him. What a hush had fallen upon the garden—there was no sound at all. It was as though some spirit had come and put a spell upon the place, leaving it white and still.

He walked softly over the snow towards the apple trees.

Now the young one stood alone, above the steps, dwarfed no longer; and with her branches spread, glistening white, she belonged to the spirit world, a world of fantasy and ghosts. He wanted to stand beside the little tree and touch the branches, to make certain she was still alive, that the snow had not harmed her, so that in the spring she would blossom once again.

She was almost within his reach when he stumbled and fell, his foot twisted underneath him, caught in some obstacle hidden by the snow. He tried to move his foot but it was jammed, and he knew suddenly, by the sharpness of the pain biting his ankle, that what had trapped him was the jagged split stump of the old apple tree he had felled that afternoon.

He leant forward on his elbows, in an attempt to drag himself along the ground, but such was his position, in falling, that his leg was bent backwards, away from his foot, and every effort that he made only succeeded in imprisoning the foot still more firmly in the grip of the trunk. He felt for the ground, under the snow, but where he felt his hands touched the small broken twigs from the apple tree that had scattered there, when the tree fell, and then were covered by the falling snow. He shouted for help, knowing in his heart no one could hear.

'Let me go,' he shouted, 'let me go,' as though the thing that held him there in its mercy had the power to release him, and as he shouted tears of frustration and of fear ran down his face. He would have to lie there all night, held fast in the clutch of the old apple tree. There was no hope, no escape, until they came to find him in the morning, and supposing it was then too late, that when they came he was dead, lying stiffly in the frozen snow?

Once more he struggled to release his foot, swearing and sobbing as he did so. It was no use. He could not move. Exhausted, he laid his head upon his arms, and wept. He sank deeper, ever deeper into the snow, and when a stray piece of brushwood, cold and wet, touched his lips, it was like a hand, hesitant and timid feeling its way towards him in the darkness.

aphne du Maurier (1907-1989) was an English novelist and playwright known for her paranormal themes.

Seth is the cartoonist behind the semi-annual hardback series of books, *Palookaville*.

His comics and drawings have appeared in the *New York Times*, *The Best American Comics*, *The Walrus*, *The New Yorker*, the *Globe and Mail*, and countless other publications. His latest graphic novel, *Clyde Fans* (twenty years in the making), was published in the spring of 2019.

He is the subject of a documentary from the National Film Board of Canada, *Seth's Dominion*.

Seth lives in Guelph, Ontario, with his wife, Tania, and their two cats, in an old house he has named "Inkwell's End."

Originally published in 1952 in Great Britain by Victor
Gollancz Ltd. in *The Apple Tree: A Short Novel and Several Long
Stories*.

Published in Great Britain in 2004 by Virago Press, an imprint
of Little, Brown Book Group, in *The Birds & Other Stories*.

Originally published in 1953 in the United States by Doubleday
and Company in *Kiss Me Again, Stranger: A Collection of Eight
Stories, Long and Short*.

Illustrations and design © Seth, 2019

Library and Archives Canada Cataloguing in Publication

Title: The apple tree / Daphne du Maurier, Seth.
Names: Du Maurier, Daphne, 1907-1989, author. |
Seth, 1962- illustrator.
Description: Series statement: Christmas ghost stories |
Originally published as part of a collection:
Victor Gollancz: London, 1952.
Identifiers: Canadiana (print) 20190115726 |
Canadiana (ebook) 20190115793 |
ISBN 9781771963176 (softcover) |
ISBN 9781771963183 (ebook)
Classification: LCC PR6007.U47 A67 2019 | DDC 823/.914—dc23

Readied for the press by Daniel Wells
Illustrated and designed by Seth
Proofread by Emily Donaldson
Typeset by Chris Andrechek

PRINTED AND BOUND IN CHINA